# Penny,

## the

## (Vengeful & Sweet-Toothed)

# Sprite of Pen-y-Ghent

by

## Andrew Musgrave

ISBN 13: 978-0995586826
ISBN-10: 0995586829

Lightship Guides and Publications
(lightshipguides@gmail.com)

Thanks to Pat & Paul Ramsden for their helpful advice,

and to Malcolm Kimber for his helpful co-operation.

## Lightship Guides & Publications

We planned to do some hiking
    from a scenic Yorkshire Dale,
We puzzled over maps and things
    for proper hills to scale,

Then we thought we'd found one perfect,
    it must be heaven sent,
There can't be nothing better
    than to climb up Pen-y-Ghent.

Twas a dark and broody night
    when we pitched our meagre camp,
The wind was howling wildly
    and flickering the lamp,
Thought we saw a ghost
    as we cowered in the tent,
Below the brooding outline
    of a moonlit Pen-y-Ghent.

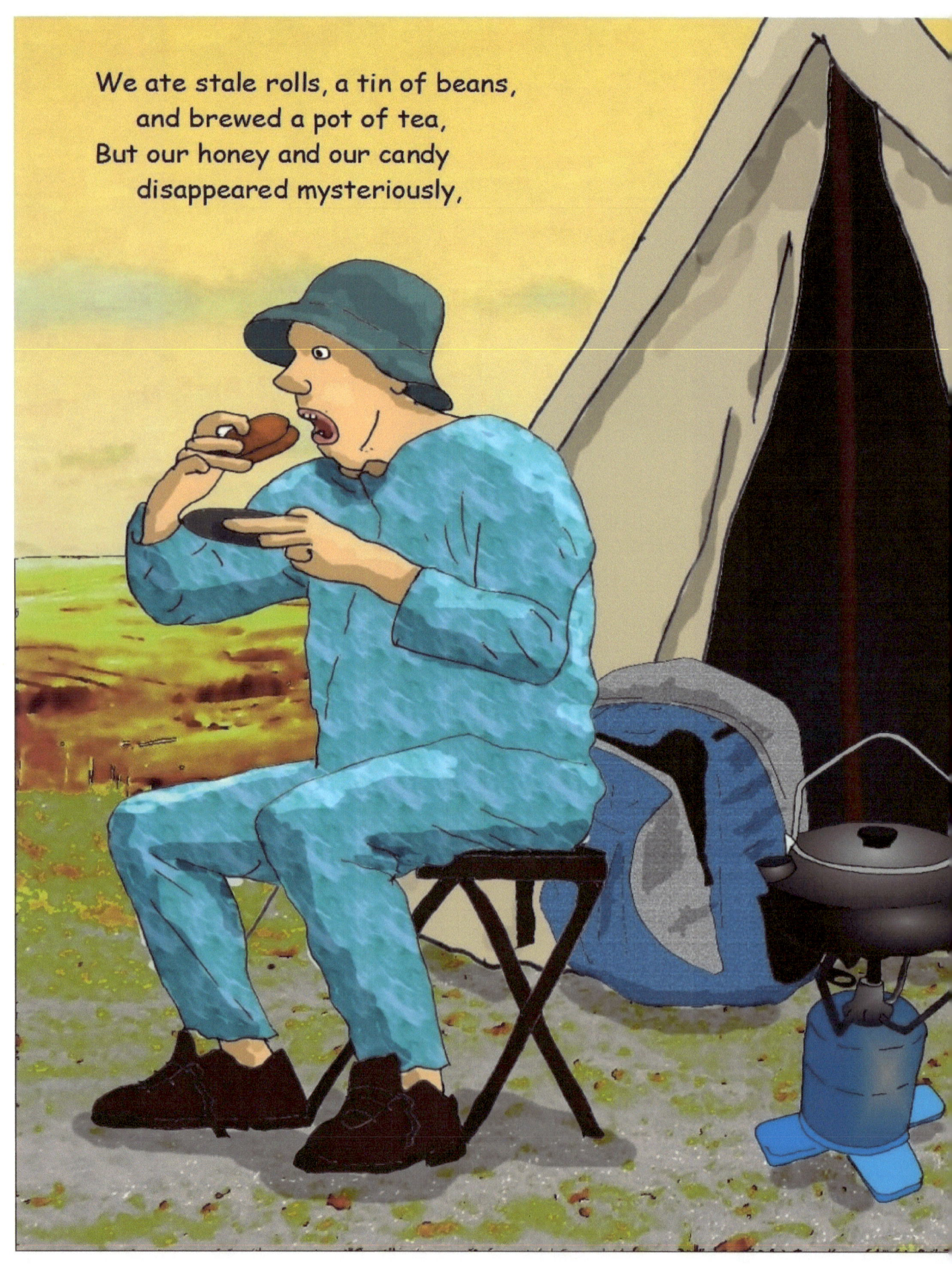

We ate stale rolls, a tin of beans,
    and brewed a pot of tea,
But our honey and our candy
    disappeared mysteriously,

We both blamed each other
for this missing abstinent
Which left us with a sour taste
for our trek up Pen-y-Ghent.

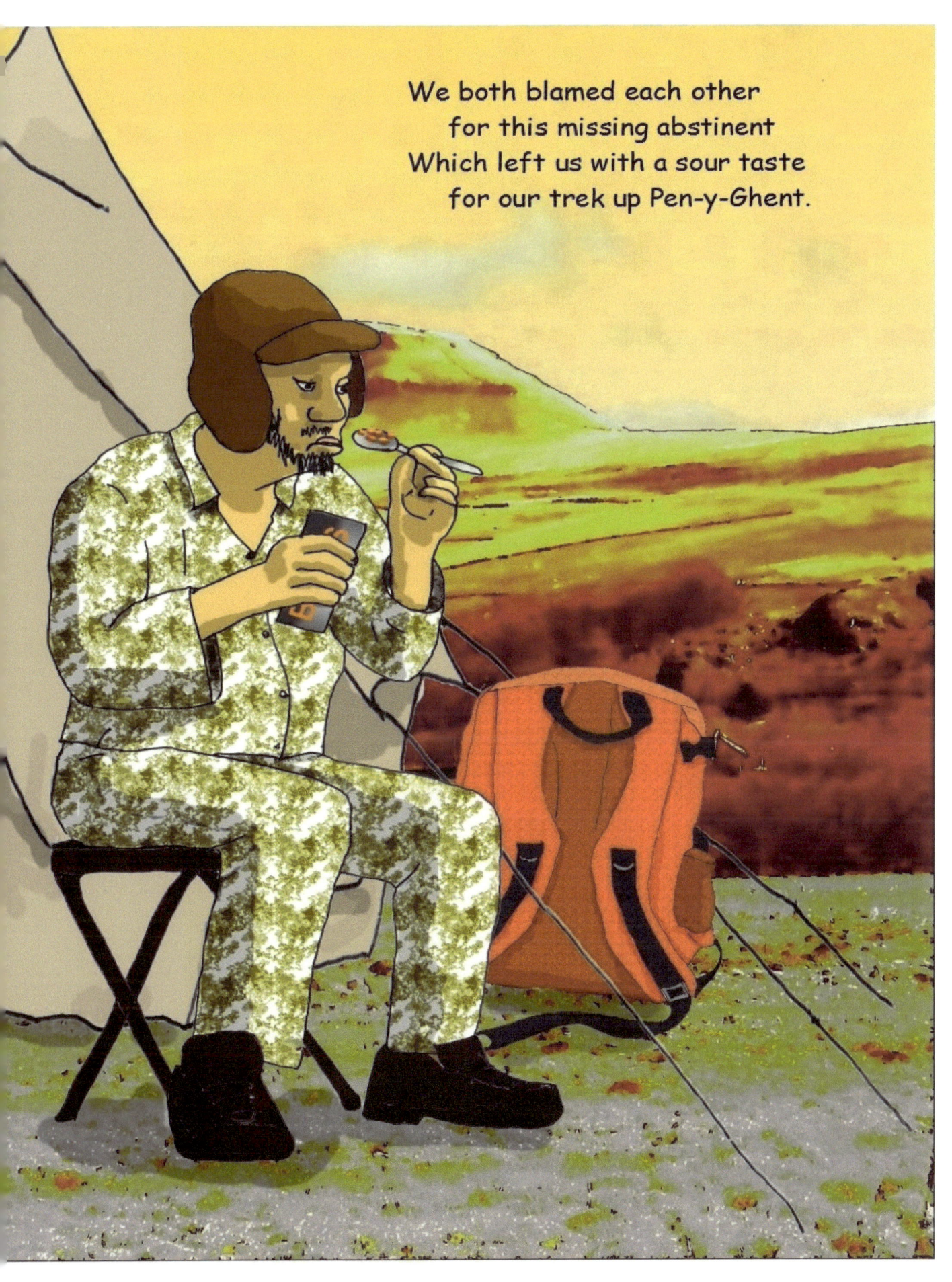

We start that fateful morning
by ambling up the track,
But we get this sort of feeling
someone else is at the back,

Something kind of sinister
is trying to prevent
Us making steady progress
on the trail up Pen-y-Ghent.

The path was getting boggy
   as we tripped across the moor,
Our legs were getting weary,
   our feet becoming sore,
The slope was getting steeper,
   but we tried to not relent
As we flailed along the flanks
   of illusive Pen-y-Ghent.

I could feel my feet get colder
   along with my toes,
A dewdrop became an icicle
   hanging from my nose,
No wild thyme or heather
   yielded fragrant scent,
On the day the rock-spirit
   walked on Pen-y-Ghent.

The clouds were getting lower,
    the mists were rolling in,
The rain was falling harder,
    the light was strangely dim,
Ahead of me a spectre made me
    think if that's what's meant
By the brooding vengeful spirit
    that haunts Pen-y-Ghent.

The crags are getting steeper,
   I'm starting to gasp,
I try to hang on tightly,
   and not release my grasp,
I feel myself get weaker,
   my energy's all spent,
Something pulls me backwards
   from the top of Pen-y-Ghent.

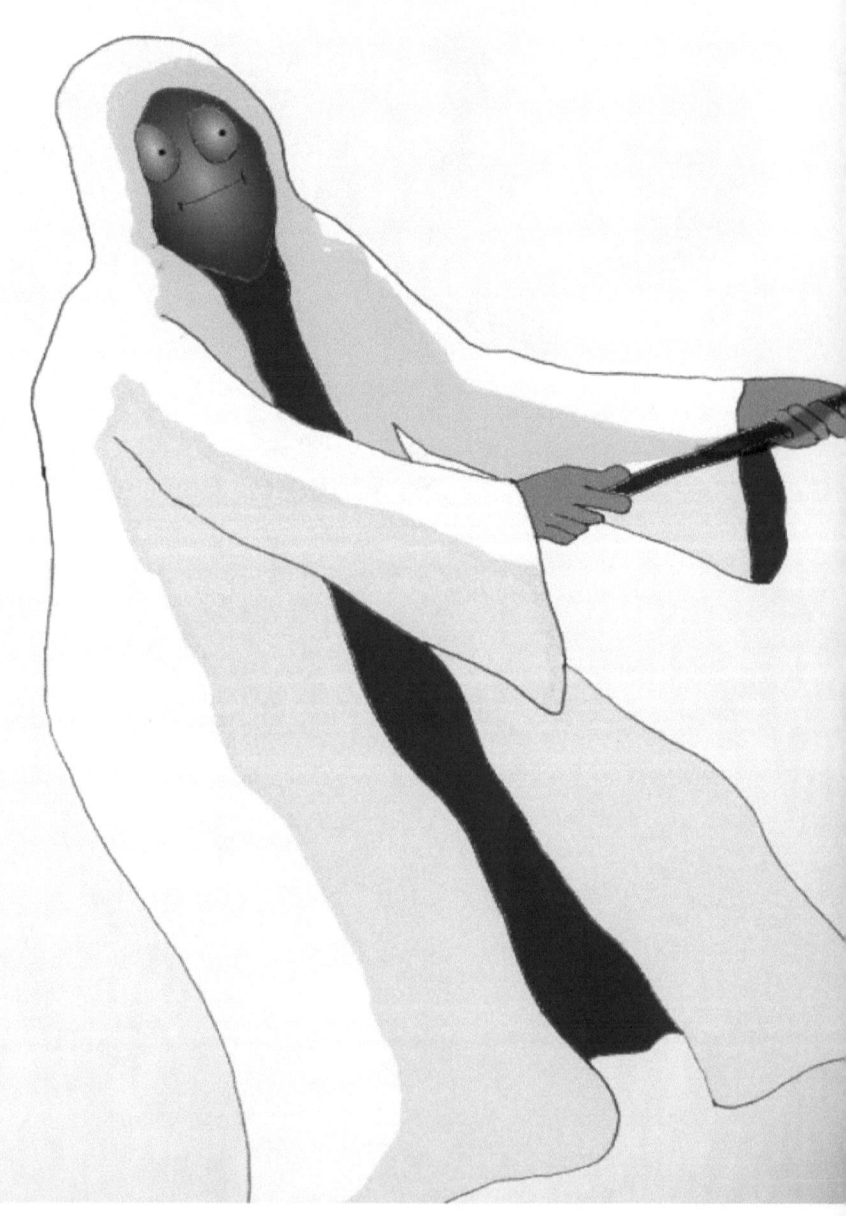

I flinch as something deadly cold
    starts grabbing at my hand,
The rocks on which I'm clinging
    are crumbling into sand,
I can hear a ghostly scream
    as the fearsome thing gives vent,
It is seeking its revenge
    for the sins on Pen-y-Ghent.

Help! I'm sliding backwards,
slipping off the scree,
I'm ripping my trousers,
grazing my knee,
My clothes are in tatters
and seem all rent,
As I'm sliding down the gullies
from the top of Pen-y-Ghent.

Showers of stones hailed downwards,
    I raced for my life,
A mile of scree pursued us:
    you bet we fled that strife!
Boulders bounced around
    us in such merriment,
And the Rock Sprite danced a jig
    atop of Pen-y-Ghent.

If it weren't so blooming scary
　　you'd have to think it funny!
This ghost, before our very eyes,
　　was spooning jars of honey!
'Twas our missing bar of mint cake
　　she took as nourishment,
And she's gobbling down <u>our</u> candy
　　while haunting Pen-y-Ghent.

*Well...*

After removing clouds of dust and brushing ourselves down
We thought we'd go sip a pint of Tetleys in *The Crown*,
There, the locals confided in a tone munificent,
'Tha's had a scrape with Penny, the Sprite of Pen-y-Ghent.'

We asked...

'What can be the motive
        for this ghoulish soul,
What makes her so intent
        to perform this fateful role?
There's got to be a reason
        she is out to augment
Her vengeful errand
        on the folks on Pen-y-Ghent.'

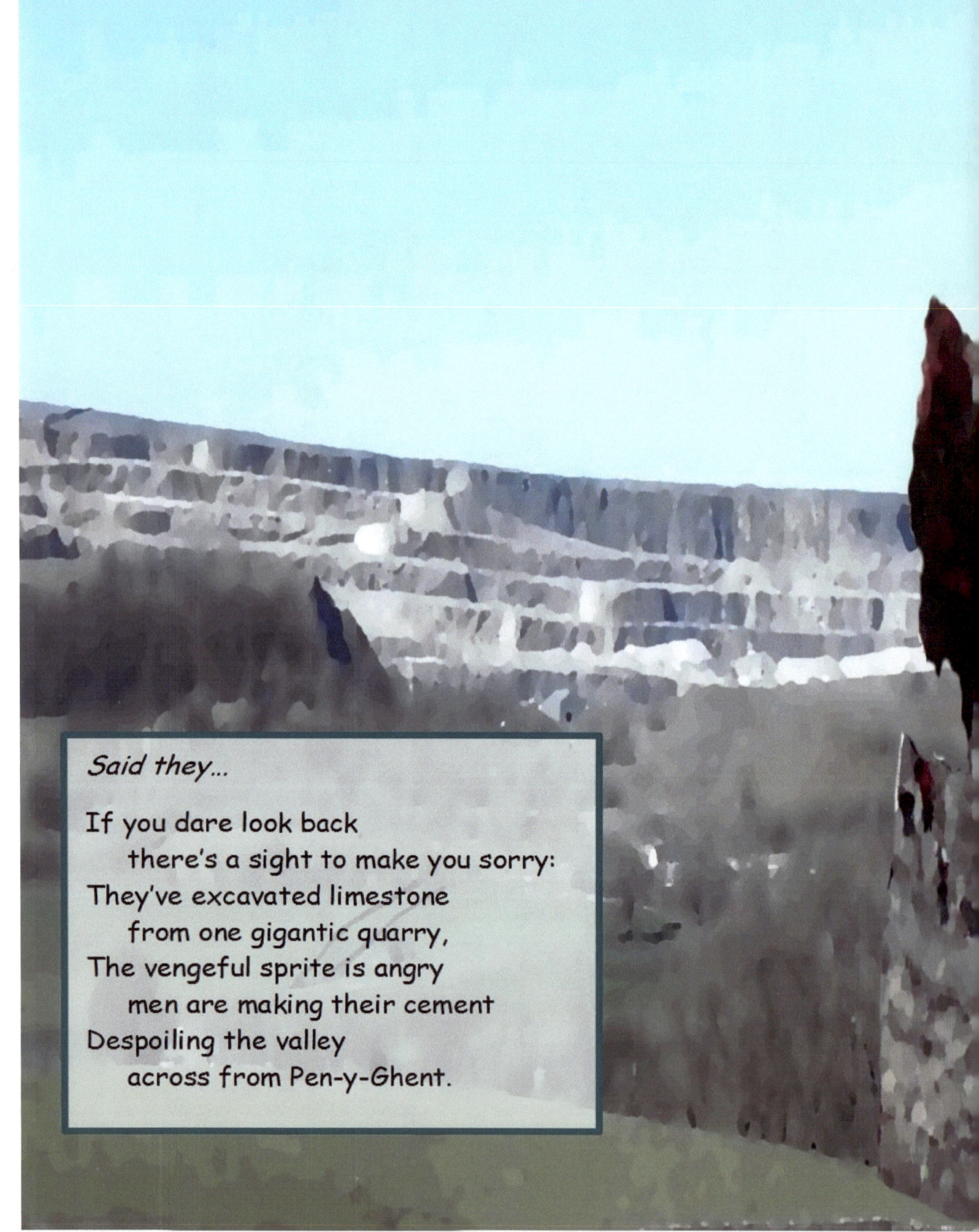

Said they...

If you dare look back
    there's a sight to make you sorry:
They've excavated limestone
    from one gigantic quarry,
The vengeful sprite is angry
    men are making their cement
Despoiling the valley
    across from Pen-y-Ghent.

Plastic bottles, tissues,
    festering banana skins,
Fag ends, pitons,
    and rusting drink tins,
It's traipsing through this litter
    that makes her vehement,
Be careful not to rile the sprite
    that stalks on Pen-y-Ghent.

So then,

Respect our bit of countryside
    whenever you roam,
Keep litter in your pocket
    until you reach your home.
Penny, she'll not harm thee
    if you be of good intent,
Oh, but bring more Kendal Mint Cake
    for your trip up Pen-y-Ghent.

Samak Fishing in Yemen

Andrew Musgrave

The book your teachers WON'T want you to read

School Anarchy

(Bad, BAD, Children)

Chris Greave

# Lightship

Guides & Publications

Ambling Along Pennine Paths

Pen-y-ghent

&

Horton in Ribblesdale

Andrew Musgrave

Orbz

How the Spider lost its wings and learnt to spin a web instead

(and how it got used to dark corners)

www.ingramcontent.com/pod-product-compliance
Lightning Source LLC
Chambersburg PA
CBHW041556120626
46551CB00002B/232